OUT OF PLACE

microfiction and prose poems

edited by

Kirsten Tranter
and Linda Godfrey

SPINELESS WONDERS
www.shortaustralianstories.com.au

Spineless Wonders

PO Box 220

STRAWBERRY HILLS

New South Wales, Australia, 2012

shortaustralianstories.com.au

First published by Spineless Wonders 2015

Cover image and design by Richard Holt

Layout by Bronwyn Mehan.

Typeset in Franklin Gothic Book

Printed and bound by Lightning Source Australia

ISBN 978-1-925052-22-0

Catalogue-in-print

A823.4

Out of Place prose poems and microfiction/

Tranter, Kirsten & Godfrey, Linda (eds)

OUT OF PLACE

microfiction and prose poems

This project has been assisted by the Australian Government through the Australia Council, its arts funding and advisory body.

Reality leaves a lot to the imagination.
JOHN LENNON

Contents

BIOGRAPHIES

EDITORS

THE JOANNE BURNS AWARD

Introduction

Throwing around ideas for a theme for this book in the microlit series, we thought *Travel*, with a capital T. Everyone loves to travel, to move, to see different things, to explore. Kirsten moves between America and Australia; Bronwyn and Linda would fly anywhere any time with anyone to be able to get away and experience the new. As we teased out the threads of what it means to travel, it was clear that the experience didn't have to be about physical movement but could also incorporate writing and reflecting on dislocation, in space, time, feeling, psyche and memory. We asked writers to interpret this theme, Out of Place, as openly, closely, fast and loosely as they liked.

What we received were stories rendered in miniature and moments inscribed with precise focus. Australia's best micro-wordsmiths produced journeys in words that took us somewhere surprising. Travels that showed us where writers started from and where they were going in a different light, newly out of place—a stolen glimpse of a father dancing alone to music; Gothic landscapes on the New South Wales coast; incredible spectrums in the colours of butterflies; Aussie cricket and climate change; remembrances of an exiled home land; a journey to give birth to a dead baby; awkward sexual politics at a funeral. The unhappiness of a couple in paradise; an animal view of human vulnerability; the taste of a thousand-year old egg, and the shape of spaghetti thrown against a wall during a fight: these stories capture delightful and unsettling moments of estrangement, when the new becomes familiar and the ordinary becomes sublime, the point when you agree to accept the strange into your own self. We'd like to make special mention of three entries we received from visitors to The Wayside Chapel, each telling their story from one place to the present day. Beautiful, poetic and a privilege to be given insight into their journeys.

Humorous, weird and breathtaking, full of laughter, irony and grace – these stories will sweep you up, shake you, stir you and set you down again somewhere other than where you began. Contributors include new authors alongside familiar voices such as renowned UK microfiction author and expat Tania Hershman, Australian microfiction queen Angela Meyer, poet John Tranter, writer Ceridwen Dovey, previous contributors to microfiction collections Susan McCreery and Mark Smith, and academics/authors and microlit aficionadas Shady Cosgrove and Moya Costello.

As with other collections much of the work for this book is done online, but sitting around a table remains a central creative space, this time in a cafe in Rozelle on a hot summer's afternoon. Bron, Kirsten and Linda met, drank coffee and talked the book into being. Our aim is always to bring you the best of short, short writing and to challenge the reader to think big, to give you a taste of the possibilities of the short form and make space for your imagination to continue the journeys started here.

—Kirsten Tranter & Linda Godfrey, 2015

Tim Heffernan

BUTTERFLIES IN IRAQ

there are no butterflies in iraq he said as we were watching the one day international on a green pitch sponsored by taubman's easycoat anti-bacterial wall paint. and the dugongs have disappeared from the reef, he continued, because they could not live with the white bleached coral colours in vogue these days, and sea grass is so sixties. meanwhile abbots, bishops and their laity are denying that climate change and fertilizer and runoff have anything to do with perceptions that butterflies don't exist on the fertile plains of the euphrates river and that poets don't have any responsibility for saving species at risk of extinction. we watch the paint dry during the ad break worried about australia's position in this game, but reassured that the government has come up with a plan involving the cricketers, the painters and the butterflies to produce a colour card that will be accessible in any bunnings from cairns to wagga with all the colours of the reef ready for walls in lounge rooms, bedrooms, and with the addition of an anti-fungal additive, in wet areas such as the kitchen, the bathroom and the great barrier reef.

Julie Chevalier

FLASH FICTION RULE #1

the month the second astronaut landed on the moon i dreamed about a blind japanese bicycle repairman   the night after the lecture on adjectives, the avoidance of   on my bike i free-wheeled down a greener-than-picture-book hill   swerved right into what might have been a deep sea fisherman's hut   had we not been landlocked   to show respect to the visually-impaired i shuffled my bike along as humbly as i shuffled my suitcase in a baggage queue   the blind japanese bicycle repairman & his seeing-eye dog, china plate, joined saturday morning tai chi at callan park   the hut-like repair shop was reassembled where thousands of bike riders passed daily   megs (who resented cyclists hogging the narrow streets of the inner west) gave the japanese man a hand-up by sprinkling thumb tacks over bike stencils on the tarmac   an astronaut issued a global alert: avoid cycling paths in rozelle new south wales australia megs texted him thanks & moon cakes   the japanese bicycle repairman's business failed   he & china plate fell in love with a former astronomy teacher who maintained her own unicycle.

Ceridwen Dovey

MIDNIGHT IN MOZAMBIQUE

It was neap tide – a low high tide, a complicated idea. Sun, earth, moon at right angles, gravity's dance out of whack. How had the first mapper of the moon, the one before the two Jesuits, described the Earth? The sublunar world. Two worlds facing each other, land masses mirrored back: one unchanged, one that churned and boiled and froze.

No light came from the fishing village. Another blackout, or else everyone – her husband too – was asleep. That morning, a local had butchered a coconut for their pleasure on this spot on the sand. None of it could save them. They had been unhappy under the palms bent sideways by wind, unhappy as they ate warm scallops on their natural shell saucers.

The moon was so bright it hurt her eyes. She felt closer to the people of the past, whose nights had been darker than anything she could imagine, whose moon had seemed brighter.

Then she shivered. The ancients had not believed the moon to be trustworthy; it was two-faced, its light dangerous. It would forever taunt women like her – moving farther away, then closer to the earth again, over billions of years. Tidal evolution, gravity's slow dance.

Kirsten Tranter

COPENHAGEN

With feet the mermen aren't even technically mermen at all. They stand there under the surface of the canal, arms upstretched, faces tilted so it's impossible to meet their eyes under the green of the water. The whole city gives up on metaphor, except for the opera house, prow forward into the canal. Serpents wind their way, literally, down the turret spire. Prepositions give me the most trouble: to you, for her, under the photograph, on the stairs, against/angst. Who are they reaching to? To whom are they reaching? My own arms ache: how tiring it would be to stand there like that for so long, a rock under water. We walk for miles by the boathouse, not embracing. I see, and turn away, green, green.

Angela Argent

LEAVING

Stopped at the smouldering red light, the kids noticed her first. It was five a.m. and they said she must feel cold standing outside the Tube like that. She looked grim.

Cranky. We didn't feel like leaving. Inside the car was T-shirt warm. Fish and chips with vinegar, the scent on their clothes. '*Wo, wo, wo your boat*,' they sang, mimicking a rhotic voice they'd heard yesterday. Cruel little bastards.

I clutched my coffee, my consolation for leaving. Through the window I watched the policewoman stride forward. Furious. She rapped at my window.

'Concentrate, woman! Hands on the wheel,' she bellowed. 'You've the safety of your young ones to consider.'

The giggling grew louder. The kids knew our car was the wrong way round for London. I was sitting in the passenger seat where the driver belonged, their dad on the left side, our mad chauffeur spinning the steering wheel with cavalier glee. Messing with her.

The policewoman peered at the Czech number plates, the oversized child at the misplaced wheel, the mountain of stuff in the back and all the other signs of delinquency. Her shrug was disparaging.

'Mind how you go,' she muttered, certain we wouldn't understand.

Shady Cosgrove

DIM SUM

The meals: sometimes I guzzle tea to keep from gagging and then I'm surprised by raw dough with sesame seed paste inside. Beautiful. The green bean ice water dessert is bizarrely gritty, unpleasant. Chicken claws outstretched on a plate: wow. Then fried dough that's like eating fairy ribbons.

But I'm stumped at the 1000-year-old egg. It's been marinated in dirt. The yolk is black, the egg white is amber. I only know it's an egg because my new friend is telling me so.

'You must try it,' she says.

I'm not an adventurous eater. I've surprised myself so far – but this is too much. I know me. The egg won't make it from fork to mouth.

'I used to eat it as a child. Every two weeks.' She is leaning close, her hair pinned back in elaborate twists. I understand what she's saying: food is culture, culture is people, the person in front of me is her.

I push the fork into my mouth, the marinated egg that is both egg and not-egg at the same time. It's salty, with traces of tea and yolk. Not unpleasant. She watches as I swallow. My fork reaches down again. I have no idea who I am.

Seabird Brooks

PILGRIM'S DREAM

I awoke from a dream about a friend I hadn't seen in years to the sound of somebody calling my name. I had no idea where I was at first, and then the word 'Nina' was said again and I realised I was in a hostel in Peru, in a city whose name I couldn't pronounce, and that somewhere across from me in the dark was an Italian guy I'd spoken to for less than five minutes in the hallway. He repeated my name once more, quieter this time, before continuing on in what I guessed to be Italian – speaking groggily, mumbling, obviously asleep. And it occurred to me then that the two of us hadn't exchanged names, that the Nina he was calling to wasn't me and that somewhere in the world there was a woman who shared my name, a woman with an entire life story behind her, a whole history of love and heartbreak and happiness and loss, and in the foggy half-light of my consciousness I thought about that woman, tried unattainably to imagine who she was and what she might be doing here, in this unfamiliar room, still haunting another pilgrim's dreams.

Ashley Haywood

THE PLOT

Sound of scrubbing stone is the sound of a cemetery in Paris on the first day of spring. Row after row, bright, plastic gloves move in unison. No one pauses for springtime disturbances: no one misses a beat for the bucket-less stranger passing through, or for the cat that tiptoes over one of the lost ones, one of the nameless and dateless sarcophagi. A break in its sandstone slab runs across the middle like a magician's act. The cat puts its nose between the thin crack, and sniffs something hidden beneath the stone, down in the undercroft. With my first step, the cat scampers, and, in my periphery, heads begin to rise. One gloved hand at a time, the *sch-sch-sch* slows to a stop. They are watching as my fingertips spell out the almost wordless engravings, and loop around the figures of a date. They are watching, pricked noses. The grave smells like homemade soap, and the cemetery goes *sch-sch-sch*.

Ali Jane Smith

RACOSPERMA

The mezzanine above uncatalogued storage has become the breakout area for the Congress of Botanists. Though divided by the reclassification of acacias, the confreres are as one in their desire for coffee, tea, reconstituted juice. Over the fragile balance of friands and mini-danish on saucers some continue their taxonomic battle, but most share news of children or commiserate over the whittling of departments.

Walking home through long grass is a good time to consider the problem of *Bidens Pilosa*, Farmer's Friends, hedgehogging socks, bootlaces and jumper. The sock guard has its limits. Looking forward to an evening in front of the tele with a glass of wine and a good strong light over the shoulder, pick pick pick, collecting the long, barbed seeds in the lid of an empty jam jar to throw in the fire. The meditative pick pick pick.

Bronwyn Shirley

MIMOSA PIGRA

'A weed,' she said, re-plaiting her thinning locks, 'is just a plant out of place.'

'Or rather,' I said, 'in its place, considering that surrounding conditions allow it to spread.'

'Well … yes … looking at it from the plant's point of view and not the person's garden that it's overtaking.' She scooped up the plaits, fastening them in a halo around her head, revealing dark purple bruises on thin arms.

'And sometimes,' I added, 'it's actually quite an attractive plant, which is why it's introduced into the garden in the first place.'

A nurse enters; takes her blood pressure, temperature, blood sugar levels.

'When's the next test?' I break the clinical silence.

'They're giving me a break for the weekend.' She shifts painfully in the bed. 'If it can shrink another 20% and if it hasn't spread anywhere else...' She started to slur and her swollen eyelids drooped.

I kept chattering on about Lantana, Mimosa, Paterson's Curse. Then, when I was sure she'd nodded off, I replaced the water in the vase, disposing of the dying Gerbera stalks, tidied and trimmed the longer-lasting white Liliums. Were these a weed? I'd seen them proliferating around sand dunes at local beaches; pretty, but insidious.

John Tranter

LETITIA'S LITHE LIMBS

As Letitia's lithe limbs slid into the tepid, prawn-coloured waters of the Gulf of Mexico, Sebastian blew a lazy plume of lilac-tinted smoke into the air and reflected on what had brought him to this god-forsaken fishing village with a suitcase full of Bolivian notes and a frightful hangover: he remembered his childhood home in the Sydney Harbourside suburb of Balmain — half a world away, and half a lifetime away! — the noisy hippy neighbours and their cacophony of old Leonard Cohen songs, the constant scent of burning dope in the air, and the lush fern in the front garden, its drooping green fronds seeming to imitate the fern pattern of the iron-lace-fronted verandah so that at times he was hard put to distinguish the tender, verdant fern from the cast-iron imitation ... God, it seemed too out of place, so out of reach ... but there was Letitia, swimming back and forth, her limbs chopping the water into frothy wavelets ... now he remembered ... that night with Letitia ... best not remembered too clearly ... Bolivian notes ... of course, the largest denominations are the largest in the world, immensely useful to drug cartels and their travelling mules and donkeys...

Richard Holt

AFLOAT

My uncle arrived at a distant archipelago on a raft he'd made from flooring offcuts and bamboo poles from Bunnings. He stumbled into reception at the Hideaway resort asking – please – if they had anything for sunburn ... only he had no money on account of his wallet going overboard during the storm.

The storm went through two days ago, said the clerk.

That long? said my uncle.

Where'd you come from? The clerk tugged the collar of his Hawaiian shirt.

Butterfield.

On the mainland! That's a hundred kilometres. Does anyone know you're here?

My uncle looked at him, a little perplexed. Well ... yes, he said. You do.

That's about when he collapsed. He came to in a luxury suite. For a few weeks, before hitching a ride home on a trawler, he was the toast of the island.

When my uncle died the people of Butterfield, a place of neatly trimmed lawns, where politeness is valued above all things, were quick to forget him.

But elsewhere his story is still joyfully told. And the people who repeat it live in a place where the water is warm and clear, the sun shines on palm-fringed beaches and nobody ever hurries.

Nick Couldwell

DANCING

Jazz plays from Dad's old record player downstairs. I hear him humming along, mumbling his words and swearing when he bumps into things. I sit up in bed and can't believe my ears; the old man is dancing. I rip the blanket off and tiptoe to the landing. I duck under the railing and look into the dingy lounge room. Dad shifts his feet across the dirty carpet in a waltz. With a ciggie dangling from his lips, he bobs and pirouettes around the coffee table like a girl's heart is on the line. He cradles his hands around plain air as if he's holding onto the dress fabric at someone's back. The record plays softly in the corner and the port in his mug shivers on the table as he moves. He weaves around the tiny flat, holding the air with a closeness I have never seen. Moths buzz in front of the light creating shadows across the chipped walls and dusty bookshelf. He keeps dancing until the record stops and it's just him, my father, breathing deeply in the middle of the room.

Angela Meyer

SPARE

Finally the dentist pulled back, sweating, and in her blood-slicked fist was my wisdom and a long sharp hook of bone. 'That's my workout for the week,' she laughed. I handed over hundreds of dollars and then filled my prescriptions.

Lea was home, with the blinds closed against the heat. 'I have a little more work to do,' she said. I took the pills and laid down on my unmade bed. She'd been sleeping in the spare room for 17 nights. My head throbbed from the pills or the pain or the heat. I should have closed the blinds, but my room poked out at the back of the house and I liked the sensation of detachment.

I dreamed of crushed cars; painkiller dreams that felt like ice scraping bone.

When the swelling had gone down, I discovered a leftover shard in my gum. When the swelling had gone down and the cool change set in, Lea left the house. I worked that shard out slowly. They kept coming. Maybe I had an extra jaw the way some people had a spare rib. I lined up the pieces on my windowsill, in my floating room, and kept the blinds open.

Bry Throssell

HOME DESIGNS SPRING CATALOGUE

I went outside with the husky, Claude, to check the mail. There wasn't any. Unless you count the *Home Designs* Spring Catalogue, which we don't. Claude peed on some things. I clipped my nails into the drain. Picked some ants off the rosebush, held them up close to my eye and crushed them between finger and thumb, before flicking them onto the road. When we turned back to the house we saw it had shrunk to the size of a bowling ball. We were certain it wasn't just a trick of the light. We knew we'd never manage to fit inside. Not even Claude alone would have fit, now that he'd decided to grow large. Our sadness over no longer being able to go inside soon passed when we realised we didn't fancy living in a house that had recently become abandoned.

Susan McCreery

SAFEKEEPING

On the way back from hospital the day my mother collapsed, I bought some leather-revitalising wax. Her handbag, which I'd taken for safekeeping despite the nurse's arched brow, was a shabby navy, the strap shot with hairline cracks.

Armed with a strip of old singlet from her cleaning cupboard, I sat down to empty it at her kitchen table. Out tumbled a coin purse, a wad of receipts bound in elastic, and a breath-freshener. In the pockets I found notepaper, a loyalty card, bent safety pins, a couple of loose pellets of gum, and a flaky headache tablet in a blister square. One by one I unrolled the receipts. All liquor outlets of various locations, some across town. Since my mouth was open, I sprayed it with spearmint and nearly choked.

I shook the bag free of grit, then proceeded to work the wax into the worn hide. Before long, it began to gleam and soften under my fingertips.

When I'd finished, I disposed of the tablet and gum and replaced the other items. I zipped the bag, then held it at arm's length, admiring, before pressing it to my face.

Venita Munir

AMPLIFICATION

Evie lies on her back. The noise-cancelling headphones squeeze her skull. Her surging thoughts press from the inside. Everyone reminds her she *has* to sleep. The relaxation CD plays but the bewitching voice and tinkling new-age music heighten her frustration.

It isn't the baby. She's pretty good, doing what's expected.

Everything is amplified.

At night, through closed doors, she can still hear the dog breathing in the hallway. Drifting doof music competes with her heartbeat. A skateboarder sounds like a freight train on the foot-path. Fruit bats arguing in the fig tree sound like pterodactyls.

He brings the baby in for a feed.

Afterwards father and daughter sleep again. Evie doesn't.

The first train triggers the boom gate's bells at 04.52 and every twenty minutes thereafter. It heralds the morning cacophony: wattlebirds choking, lorikeets shrieking, magpies gargling.

Every sound shoots an arrow of adrenaline through her body. Her vision is in pixels. Kaleidoscopic windmills twirl under her eyelids. Her chest may explode with her trapped breath.

Oh, to drop off that knife-edge into sleep.

She's made a mistake.

The baby is hers, but she wants to give it back.

Or run away.

He won't be happy either way.

Christy Collins

THE RAINS

He didn't usually speak to guests, but she was in the recreation room, damp in bathing gear and a sarong, not reading the book she held in her lap. It had rained all week and he was sorry.

'I don't mind,' she said.

'Tonight's buffet will be good, at least.'

'I'm vegetarian.'

'Well, sorry anyway.' He turned back to mopping up the rainwater.

From behind him she said, 'We should meet later. For a drink. It doesn't have to be here. You probably know a much better place.'

'No,' he said. 'Sorry.'

She frowned and opened her book.

He turned from her. He felt watched. She was attractive, but many of them were, and they were all gone after seven to nine days.

She shifted in the chair. He left then, his mop held aloft as if he was the flag bearer at the Olympics. She wondered what he thought of them all: decadent, barely-clothed Westerners.

A moment later, he returned carrying a towel. 'For your hair,' he said, then his demeanour turned serious. 'There's a local place, it's next to the Marriot. If I were to run into you there, at nine perhaps, it couldn't be helped.'

Andrea Gawthorne

A DISH SERVED

'You didn't phone.'

'I forgot.'

Not I'm sorry, but I forgot. It was their first fight.

'Date night,' she pointed to the red and brown smear on the bedroom wall. Her first slap-up meal. One thin wobble of spaghetti clung to the edge of the skirting board. A little worm of remorse.

'Don't be like that.' She smelt stale bourbon as he pulled her towards him. Over his shoulder, the stain was a map.

He brought her breakfast in bed. A cup of tea, roses from their neighbour's garden, cold spaghetti on toast.

Gillian Telford

PERFETTO

A perfect night ... corner table ... attentive waiters ... *per favore* and *grazie* flowing like the wine. But half-way through *il primo*, the mood was broken. We heard them before we saw them; a mid-life couple in matching T-shirts from Des Moines, seated where we became unwilling eavesdroppers. He removed his Lions cap and demanded translation of the menu while complaining it was not the sort of food he was used to back home in Iowa. Order placed, he set up his iPad, then read to his wife (and the rest of us) all ten of Someone's *Best Things To Do In Venice*. She said little but sat, turning a wedding band round and around her finger. By number eight ... *while nothing short of a major cliché, seeing the Grand Canal from the Rialto Bridge is just something that everyone must do* ... she laughed in a nervy, high-pitched way. Watching her, I was reminded of Rilke's angels: *They all have mouths so tired, tired...* But her husband didn't linger over his food. On leaving, he slapped his cap back on his head, remarking in somewhat baffled tones *Well, I couldn't complain about the fish*.

Matthew Gabriel

jesussaves82

Jeannie liked her men a little different, and so Jesus was perfect for her. In the flippancy and vagaries of online dating a man like Jesus got a lot of clicks, some drunken repartee, but rarely any interest. After all he dressed like Jesus, wrote like one of his apostles, and thought he actually was that other man. Yet, his imposture was too studied even for those who loved the real one. For Jeannie, an atheist, he was curious enough to warrant a chance.

He brought a bag of fish and bread to their first date: a picnic in the park. He told long-winded stories of Galilee, referred to himself in third person, and came across as too distant for Jeannie. She liked the way he dressed and he was easy on the eye, but she needed more. She told Jesus as much.

When she left, he insisted she take the fish. She could hear her kids already screaming and protesting at the dinner table, so on her way out of the park she peered over her shoulder and dumped the bag in the bin.

Tania Hershman

THE EVOLUTIONARY IMPERATIVE OF LAUGHTER IS CONFUSED

She laughed and her laughing made me nervous, I was trying to help her and didn't know: was she delighted or hysterical? I didn't want to stop trying to help her, our time was bounded, she was a stranger to me and had come; I offered services. She laughed, I pointed to her work, I laughed, and then, towards the end, as we were drawing the close closer and I had almost finished, had nothing more to say, she said, I haven't laughed so much for ages, and I said, Oh, thank goodness, I didn't know! I said, I didn't know if it was a good sign, and she laughed at that too, and she stood up and I stood up, we moved towards the door, and she was smiling and we said goodbye. I could hear her, all the way down the stairs.

Stuart McGuckin

WRONG PATH?

I'm not completely sure but I think I made a wrong turn back there. That last left should have been a right; there's a slight chance I've been reading the map the wrong way around. Also I don't think this is where I was meant to be at this point of the journey; in fact, I'm almost certain.

Maybe that last turn wasn't the mistake though; maybe I made the wrong turn much earlier ... I've probably been walking down the wrong path for a long time now without even knowing it. Actually that's not true, I think maybe I've suspected something for some time now and just haven't been willing to admit it to myself.

Do you know the funny thing? I've kept walking in spite of that, and I've continued walking while I've told you my tale. Maybe I'm not in the right spot. Maybe I'm not even remotely close but I suppose there is not much point turning back now. Might as well keep pressing ahead and see where I end up.

Katherine Temple

A LONG JOURNEY

I came across a roadside stall. I saw many different small bags of apples, oranges, onions. Every bag was two dollars.

I was surprised. It was the first time in my life I saw a roadside stall with a tin box, and the note outside the tin read, *Pay and get your own change here.*

I bought two bags of apples and two bags of oranges. Then I paid and took the change by myself as there was nobody there. I felt like I was the only person in the world. I was proud of myself and I was honoured.

It made me think of Vietnam in 1945 – bad weather, food shortages, many people died of starvation. It makes me emotional whenever I think of it and what happened to my people.

It touches my heart many years after and when I write about it today.

I also feel very fortunate.

Trinity Morris

TO GO BACK

I walked into the room full of people. I knew straight away something was not right. I said to myself *I should have stayed at home.* My tummy is turning there where people are looking at me and I felt dizzy. All I wanted to do was scream and run away and cry.

When I am at home I feel safe and comfortable and my tummy is full of butterflies and happiness.

I started to realise everywhere I go I knew it was safe but I had to leave here to feel comfortable within myself at my home and my pictures. When I am at home with my pictures all of the memories of my childhood come back and it gives me a lot of happiness.

The picture I treasure the most is me at the beach on a hot sunny day, playing in the water with my family.

I say to myself I will never feel out of place when I have this picture, it means a lot to me. It makes me feel like a better person that feels confident and happier. Then I feel good being in a room full of people. So knowing this, I decide to go back to the party.

As I open the door, feeling so much happiness within myself, something magical happens...

Robert Hannah

HARD THINKING

I have always felt out of place. Getting into trouble even though I didn't start it. I was put into welfare and went through 87 foster homes, in and out of detention centres and then in and out of jail. I became an alcoholic because of my upbringing, drinking very heavy. I almost got married three times but it never worked out because of my drinking. I became very closed off and didn't trust anyone.

I went to Melbourne to meet Debbie my ex but it failed. I got depressed and drunk and tried to kill myself. I drank and drank and drank until I started to do some real hard thinking. I thought my Grandpa would not want to look down and see me like this, let alone want me to hurt myself. So I got on Oasis and started talking to girls. I was chatting with this beautiful girl named Trinity. 12 months later I am happy. I am still with her and we are engaged to be married next year in October on my birthday.

And now I no longer feel out of place. Thank you Grandfather. Thank you Trinity. Thank you me.

Melissa Beit

A HOSPITAL BIRTH

'I'm here for a procedure.'

Three nurses look at me in synchrony. Mild interest, faint hostility, mild disinterest.

'What kind of procedure?'

For weeks I've held myself together like an armful of oranges, but they spill and go rolling all over the polished linoleum of the hospital corridor. 'An induced labour,' my husband says with a new belligerent tone, holding me upright under the arms.

My collapse is met with briskness. A midwife leads me by the elbow through corridors teeming with signs of imminent or recent birth, a nightmare scape for someone with a belly as small and unpromising as mine.

'We'll put you in here,' she says, tucking me out of sight. 'We don't want to upset the other ladies.'

Later, once labour is well under way and I'm begging her for pethidine, she mutters, 'I didn't become a midwife to go through this sort of thing.'

My other children were born at home, under water, with music playing and candles burning.

When it's over I gaze at our dead child, who resembles a miniature alien. An alien whose body is incompatible with life on earth.

'Oh,' says the midwife wistfully. 'It's a boy.'

Tess Pearson

NO SAFE PLACE

The principal called our parents and asked them to talk with us before it was announced at school. Mum switched off the stove. She used the words, 'terrible accident,' and stroked my head. The day before, I'd called him a fat loser. It wasn't me who'd called him a retard later on, but we'd all laughed when we heard him blubbering on the bus. It wasn't the first time he'd talked about doing it. The day after, someone came into school to talk about safety on trains and at stations. But he hadn't been on the train or at a station. He'd been in one of those tunnels without a nook to stand in when a train came. The following week they sent someone to talk about mental health. That was the closest to anyone saying it might have been on purpose. His mother came up to me at the funeral. Through a wobbly smile, she told me I was his best friend. What could I say? Her face was raw, her eyes tiny slits beneath huge swollen lids. I just nodded, and held her hand in mine. It was a lie, but I didn't know what else to do.

Mark Smith

LESS THAN A MINUTE

They say drowning is an easy death; you swallow water and the water swallows you.

Tahir Al Rifi, born to a land of dry wind and sand, may have thought otherwise when the waves breached the outer bank, shifted direction and swept him into the rip.

Water, like emotion, always channels somewhere.

He had only ever seen the vast blue canvas of the ocean from the plane when he crossed into Kenya and flew out of Nairobi. But here in this new land he wanted to touch the water, smell the salt on the wind and write his African name in the wet sand.

Another man – a man imprinted with a swimmer's DNA bred of long summers at the beach – would brace body and mind against the sweep, and resist. But nothing in his homeland has prepared Tahir for this force of water, the way it moves over and through him, pulling him down until he breathes it in.

His arms flail the surface, but the weight of his body, of all the sand and stone in his bones, drags him down and, in less than a minute, he is gone.

Dorothy Simmons

ON THE HOUR

you'll be on your way   you'll be walking down that corridor
setting one foot in front of the other   breathing in breathing out
listening your body what's it saying your good body blood and
bone   raced horses   felled timber hammered nails danced
jigs dripped sweat swam creeks   stamped shivered cursed
sang   held squalling babies as tenderly as bleeding men   your
body   that you'll be walking into a room it'll never walk out of
how can you do that   set one foot in front of the other   up to
the drop   look   the drop   you'll be   holding out your hands
to be pinioned   flexing your fingers long strong sinewy fingers
always kept your nails clean   now   bending your neck for that
rough collar like you bent it for me to kiss goodbye my fingers
stroking the soft hair at the nape   like they used to stroke the
soft down where the bones hadn't set your fingers were chubby
then   kneading my breast as you latched on   kneading eyes
shut bliss but open now awake wide awake under the hood
what do you see my son what do you say

die like a kelly   die like a kelly

Sarah Vincent

THE LOOKOUT

I'd like to lean on the railing but the seagulls have crapped all over it. I'd like to lean and lean and lean till I'm as flat as the ocean, till I'm nothing but a long thin line. But I can't get shit on my new suit. I wanted a grey one but you wear black to a funeral, don't you? And you stand up straight.

When I was little I used to beg to walk this railing. Dad would say *it's old and dirty and it's not safe* but Mum would say *what's the worst that can happen?* and she'd lift me up.

I look over at Dad. He hasn't even gotten out of the car. He's sitting there just staring out at nothing so I climb up. It shakes but it holds me. Some lady down on the sand looks up at me. What's her problem? Hasn't she ever seen a guy in a suit at the beach standing on a wooden fence shouting fuck you to the sky? I get down and get back in the car. Dad looks at my pants but doesn't say anything. He starts the engine for the long ride home.

Angela Smith

A WAKE

I'm overdressed in Melbourne black among a suntanned crowd of flirty dresses and short shorts.

'Spread a little love,' says the MC. 'Give the person next to you a hug.'

My cousin: hard drinker, failed property developer; his legacy a teenage bride and a half-built subdivision of salmon-pink mansions skirting a man-made lake.

We used to pedal Brisbane streets, chucking newspapers onto lawns at dawn, sneaking coins from Uncle John's till for our trouble. At dusk, Dad and Uncle John argued politics on the veranda, Auntie Joan refilling their glasses. Dad giving her a look he never gave Mum.

Charles D'Anastasi

THE BROKEN HOUSE

After his wife was killed in the last air raid, he went around in a daze wearing her glasses, even some of her clothes. At one of the remaining windows of the half-demolished house, the sky, abandoned by all but a few stars, held the hour. He reasoned that only this darkness allowed him such strange stillness, where so many things became possible. He remembered how he used to stand next to her as she hung the clothes on the line, and how in a childlike manner he would hand her the pegs one by one. It did not matter that sometimes, between them, words were knocked down awkwardly, like glasses of spilt wine.

Now, he struggled to make sense of the open-ended silence that lay ahead. Again and again, he would revisit their not so distant past: an austere hotel room, dimly lit corridors, a concertina of scratched music, flesh negotiations in the afternoon.

He moved through the rubble, conjoined to the hour's slow burn, where memories continued to breathe in, breathe out, almost convinced it had to be her sobs in the next room that clung to him like a wet shirt. And in the sky, stars shivered.

Lisa Smithies

GERT BY SEA

It started with a postcard, forty-two years ago, of the most exotic beach Gertrude Jones had ever seen, with jet black sand and a teal sea. Since then, every afternoon, Gert stood at her kitchen sink, looked out the window and dreamt of this moment, here and now, sitting on this beach in Santorini. In the time it took her to wash the dishes, she painted herself into the picture, only stopping when she happily heard Roger's Holden coming down the gravel drive.

The Holden paid for this trip. She didn't want to sell it, but didn't want to watch it rust either.

She used to invent different scenarios, but for the last year it was always just as it is now. Sitting on the navy and white striped towel, in the red polka dot one-piece, the broad brimmed hat, looking out to that sea. Even the breeze is exactly as she imagined it.

The only difference is the sand.

Which is not actually sand, but small dark pebbles.

She doesn't mind though, because, when she shuts her eyes and moves her feet, just so, it almost sounds like the tyres of an old Holden coming down a gravel drive.

Haider Catan

PURPLE BREEZE

for my grandmother

at ash season, a rustling of fronds in my chest could be a smidgen from the last dream. a smoky breeze, a friendly ghost, behind blazing hills dashing along, accelerating, such an unbridled horse, the bushes of purple i know are carrying the scent of your cardamom. in the southern rain-ash-forest, i walked with the smell of ashes in my nostrils. it trembled my bones and flustered my heart. *no worries, mate. It's the terror wild-fire, reconciles us with the bloody promised hell. no worries, mate. it's pure wood, war-iron free, the innocent nature takes a little killing, mate.* local aussie talk. how could you not adore their words? that smooth nasal twang. full of no worries, mate. suicide eucalyptus have exploded, the smoke season's gone, see foliage again. purple falls into peaceful slumber; extends itself with fingers towards the sky, praying for peace. the sun throws its sash to dry tears of greenery. oh my love! lately we recognised how ungrateful we were. oh you! i do remember your woody purple, your teapot, puffing your cigarette, heartbreak. oh my dear! your pure purple again, your terror, your endangered smile again. so when i hear my nickname, *hudooish*, i recognise why this name tastes of wood and salty tears in my mouth.

Moya Costello

NORTHERN RIVERS: A GOTHIC TALE

To come to Northern Rivers is to find – or lose – yourself among vines, beneath trees, under rain shatter, in flood-marked houses on stilts, within storms of deep, low thunder, high ice-green clouds and lightning startle.

Rivers flow and twist across the land like the snakes of the region do, appearing, disappearing, but remaining a felt presence – bright green and midnight-blue, red-bellied, copper and diamond-skinned – as if the land is theirs. And it is.

To come to Northern Rivers is to come to rainbow colour. A bright, neon-lime green, a satiated black, regular grey-white mornings and evening mist, and the soft baby-blue blanket of sky. The sky could have merged with the land, forgetting the horizon, but for the dark ranges.

Homelessness: a vertiginous sensation; suspension over a fathomless space. You can disappear in the rainforest, in this place of extremes, of precipitous hills in impossible lushness, of khaki lizards, tarnished-silver skinks, flat-padded geckos, large black and fast-jumping orange spiders, laughing kookaburras, curious wallabies, wary koalas, intrepid echidnas, and butcher birds with sharp phrasings that could be warnings, anger, or half-songs, a tilting in the ether of bell notes, incomplete and resonant.

Here, in this overwrought place, you might fall. You might float. You might fly.

Roberta Lowing

SOUTH

In the centre of the lake, the black heron lifts its head and listens. Beyond the wind worrying the shore are silent caves littered with rusted cans, jammed cameras, grenades. On the ridge, trees tremble, their leaves filled with fog; the nodes of orange lichen on their trunks are worn copper coins. The heron looks west, beyond vast pools latticed with telegraph wires, to the neat and unassuming corrugated roofs that swim against backyard cemeteries. To the north are classrooms stilled by holes of light, tennis shoes filled with green water, mossy humps of cars at rest beneath mouldy silhouettes of chimneys. To the east: vivisected computers rock like broken shells in tributaries as grey as the vine-wreathed tank that creaks in the gum tree. The heron listens. Between the lap-and-clink of martini shakers and television valves, the wind from the south carries a rustle of pages. It is the fall of the last calendar from the last kitchen wall, the scattering of unheeded seasons, technicolour ashes across granite water.

Barnaby Smith

VOLUNTEER

The flies are slow here, and easy to kill. I could stroke them if I wanted. I analyse flies because I am too tired to go outside, and I have been too tired since not long after the appointment. I am too tired to sing out when some aimless rambler strolls below, so I lie down in silence, until I hear only silence. A few times there has been a scream when they reach it. The scream affects my bowels and nothing more, and I am heavy most of the time, so it is welcome. I think more and more about why I took the appointment, and today I believe that, on some level, I wanted to become tired and heavy. What more than shelter do you need when you are tired and heavy? No traumas hurt you if you are tired. I smell foul, and have lost two pieces from my solitaire set, but I am fulfilled. Now, for example, I will lie here until I must take some water, then I will kill two flies I have been watching. It is too late for anyone to pass now, although I imagine half the world will arrive tomorrow.

Pip Smith

SKINS

A horse, a fox, a dog and a hen were looking in the lit window of a farmer's house. He was washing his beard in a basin full of orange-scented milk with his eyes pinched shut. They did not recognise him. They saw that the walls were hung with heads on boards, and the floor was covered with skins. They didn't recognise him because he, too, had taken off his skin and had hung it on the back of a chair. The farmer stood up from the basin and they saw that his face was pink like a possum before it opens its eyes.

He caught sight of them outside his window, standing one on top of the other like a nativity set stacked away in January. He turned to face them with his razor in his hand. They stood stacked on each other's backs; their eyes black and full; the hair on their necks standing up like proud collars.

Outside, the dew turned to frost. *At least we have our skins*, thought the fox, *but he will freeze to death*.

Rjurik Davidson

OTHERWORLD

I once wandered here with eyes like black saucers, my hair wild and windswept. Car headlights moved on both sides of me, like Chinese lanterns in the night. When I reached the other side (where we are now) I felt the swish of the cars behind me. Life can be dangerous, but you can't worry about it. You need to live your life, see, as a piece of art.

I can see that you're frightened, but come with me through this door. Look up overhead, where golden circles spin like brilliant fireflies in the night. They make your heart skip, like fireworks over the river on a summer's night.

The usual rules don't apply here, to the walls that shift like barriers in our mind. They don't apply to the creatures that bite down on concepts, swallowing them as if they were morsels of bread. They can eat you up, those creatures, and steal your very thoughts.

Come closer. Oh, you're so dry! Your skin is like parchment, like canvas almost. Your bones, just wood nailed together. Don't run away. Why, how light you are, as I raise you up against the wall, just so! And finally you're not afraid, and you shouldn't be. You have your place now, don't you?

Stephanie King

CHUCK CLOSE

The subject of his portraits was the portrait itself. She tried to take in the black sans serif from the white white as he shadowed her through the exhibition, pretending to read, inhaling, pressing his heat, too close. It was the beautiful book, the necklace, his grandmother's hat; each gesture more lovely than the next, and innocent, the things needing homes. Like the sprawling aloe vera that had outgrown its pot and did have to be split, uprooted, replanted, tended.

Named. All his things had names, Wanda, Ava, Jean – a car, a decanter, a board – and each had its place, although the flat was not yet a week old and still reeked of paint. She had wondered where the boxes were, but forgot quickly, falling willingly onto the divan.

He caught up with her in the room of *Keith*, the series of imperfect mezzotints, impossible in their scope to communicate seamlessly from copper to paper. The mouths all appeared worn out, printing lighter from too many proofs, from wear to the lips at the centre of the plate. She'd not seen this black before, this mezzotint black, and said so. He took her finger, scored a word on the plaque – *velvety* – and suggested sushi.

Biographies

ANGELA ARGENT has begun an MCA at UTS and used to live in the Czech Republic. She has published in *Seizure*, *Pilcrow &Dagger*, *Swamp*, *Gender and History* and various feminist anthologies and is writing a novella set in Prague.

MELISSA BEIT'S short fiction has been published in *Southerly*, *Meanjin*, the *Sleepers Almanac*, *Best Australian Stories*, *New Australian Stories*, *Skive* Magazine and the *Australian Women's Weekly*. She lives in coastal northern NSW with her family and a bunch of chooks.

SEABIRD BROOKS is a scribbler from the South Coast of NSW. His fiction has appeared in *Tincture*, *Seizure* and *Verity La*. In 2014 he was awarded runner-up in the Josephine Ulrick Literature Prize.

HAIDER CATAN grew up in Iraq. He is a PhD student of Psychology at UOW. Haider enriched his experience of poetry & writing in English by working with Tim Heffernan, reading at Rocket Readings and translating for The Red Room.

JULIE CHEVALIER's third book, *Darger: his girls*, won the Alec Bolton Prize and was short-listed for the Western Australian Premier's Poetry Prize. Recently she co-edited *Cracking the Spine: ten Australian Short Stories and How They Were Written*.

CHRISTY COLLINS has worked in research centres, universities and academic publishing in Australia and the Netherlands. She currently lives in Melbourne, with her husband, and is completing a PhD at the University of Tasmania.

SHADY COSGROVE is the author of *What the Ground Can't Hold* (Picador, 2013) and *She Played Elvis* (2009), which was shortlisted for the Australian Vogel Award. Her short fiction has appeared in *Best Australian Stories*, *Overland*, *Antipodes* and *Southerly*.

MOYA COSTELLO teaches writing in the School of Arts and Social Sciences, Southern Cross University. She has two collections of short prose and two novellas. She has work in Spineless Wonders' *Small Wonder*, *Stoned Crows* and *Writing to the Edge*.

NICK COULDWELL is a twenty-five-year-old writer from Byron Bay. His fiction has been published in *Visible Ink*, *Seizure*, *Westerly*, Spineless Wonders' *Writing to the Edge* and their Slinkies e-Singles edition. Nick won the 2015 Joanne Burns Award.

CHARLES D'ANASTASI is a Melbourne poet. He was the winner of the first Spineless Wonders' prose poems & microfiction competition 2012. His chapbook *Madame Bovary and other prose poems* was published by Mark Time Books in 2014.

RJURIK DAVIDSON has written short stories, essays, reviews and screenplays. His latest book is the fantasy, *Unwrapped Sky*. Rjurik can be found at www.rjurik.com and tweets as @ rjurikdavidson.

CERIDWEN DOVEY is the author of the novel *Blood Kin*, and the short story collection *Only the Animals*. She also writes non-fiction for *The Monthly* and *The New Yorker* online.

MATTHEW GABRIEL lives and works in Melbourne. He is currently completing a Masters in Creative Writing at Adelaide University. He writes short stories.

ANDREA GAWTHORNE lives in the NSW Southern Highlands. She believes that short is definitely sweeter and is currently turning all her half-finished novels into short stories and her short stories into flashers.

ASHLEY HAYWOOD has recently completed her PhD thesis, *Harlequin Blue and The Picasso Experiment*. She is a nomadic writer, editor and painter.

TIM HEFFERNAN was born on the banks of the Murrumbidgee River and worked his way upstream. Now coastal, he sometimes feels out of place – which has been good for his writing, work and family. He is a serial spineless wonder.

TANIA HERSHMAN, who holds dual UK-Australian citizenship, is the author of two story collections: *My Mother Was An Upright Piano: Fictions* (Tangent Books, 2012), and *The White Road and Other Stories* (Salt, 2008), co-author of *Writing Short Stories: A Writers' & Artists' Companion* (Bloomsbury, 2014), and curator of the ShortStops online short story hub. taniahershman.com

RICHARD HOLT coordinates *Flashing the Square*, which produces microfiction for public video display. His blog (bigstorysmall.com) needs work, because his laptop has disappeared under mountains of domestic mess. He designed the cover of this book.

STEPHANIE KING is a writer and performer from Sydney. She has written for *Crikey*, *Cordite*, *Writ*, Radio National and the forthcoming *Press* anthology. She has edited two UTS anthologies and has a play in development with Playwriting Australia.

ROBERTA LOWING is the author of two collections of poetry, *Ruin* (IP Press) and *The Searchers* (Island Press), and the novel *Notorious*, shortlisted for the Commonwealth and Prime Minister's Literary Awards.

SUSAN MCCREERY is a writer and proofreader from Thirroul, NSW. She was awarded a Varuna Fellowship and an ASA mentorship for her short story collection. She is working on a collection of microfiction.

STUART MCGUCKIN likes words. He likes them so much that when asked he claims to be a writer. He is not sure if that's a legitimate claim or not but for now he's sticking by it.

ANGELA MEYER is the author of a collection of flash fiction, *Captives* (Inkerman & Blunt), and the editor of *The Great Unknown* (Spineless Wonders). She has widely published both fiction and nonfiction, and is working on a novel. literaryminded. com.au @LiteraryMinded

VENITA MUNIR is a Melbourne based writer, studying

Professional Writing and Editing at RMIT University. She is enjoying a hiatus from her former career, as an emergency specialist, to pursue her passion for writing.

TESS PEARSON is a Sydney-based writer who works in the mental health and community sector. She is currently working on a research project on trauma, which straddles the worlds of literature and neurobiology.

A law student at University of Technology, Sydney, **BRONWYN SHIRLEY** lives in Canberra, swims with manta rays and is preparing a collection of micro-noir fiction. 'Life is too short for more than 200 words.'

Moving from Northern Ireland to Australia, **DOROTHY SIMMONS** is now a teacher and writer. Her publications include four YA novels, short fiction, poetry and essays; her novel *Living Like A Kelly* is due out later this year.

ALI JANE SMITH is a poet and critic. Her work has appeared in *Southerly, Cordite, Famous Reporter* and other journals. She is the author of the chapbook *Gala* (Five Islands Press 2006). She lives in Wollongong, Australia.

ANGELA SMITH writes poetry and flash fiction. Her poetry has appeared in many literary journals. Angela has been awarded a number of Varuna Residencies including a Second Book Fellowship.

BARNABY SMITH is a journalist, musician and poet currently based in northern New South Wales. His poetry has appeared in *Best Australian Poems, Cordite, Southerly* and others. He also writes for *Rolling Stone Australia*, ABC Arts and the *Guardian*, and is one half of music duo Telegraph Tower.

MARK SMITH'S writing has been published widely in journals, anthologies and magazines including *Best Australian Stories*, *Great Ocean Quarterly* and *The Australian*. He won the 2015 *Josephine Ulrick Literature Prize*. He lives, surfs and occasionally works on Victoria's west coast. He has just completed his first novel.

PIP SMITH is a writer and devisor of writing-based events. Her first poetry collection, *Too Close for Comfort* won the inaugural Helen Ann Bell Award and was published by Sydney Uni Press in 2013. She is currently writing a novel-in-a-box about the various personas of Eugenia Falleni (1875-1938).

LISA SMITHIES writes short fiction and screenplays. She teaches creative writing at the University of Melbourne, where she is completing a PhD that examines why the human brain loves short fiction. She runs the blog Creative Writer PhD.

GILLIAN TELFORD is a NSW Central Coast poet who enjoys regular dislocation. Her second collection of poems, *An Indrawn Breath*, was assisted by a 2014 Varuna/ Picaro Press PIP Fellowship and published in May, 2015.

KATHERINE TEMPLE is a 45-year-old woman who was born in Vietnam before emigrating to Australia in 1998. She is passionate about community and has been a regular visitor of the Wayside Chapel for over two years.

BRY THROSSELL is an emerging writer and designer from

Melbourne. At the age of 16 she won an Fellowship of Australian Writers' young writers prize for poetry and has accomplished very little since in the way of publication. Currently working in evidence preparation, she hopes to one day write something longer than a paragraph.

JOHN TRANTER has published over twenty collections of verse. His collection *Urban Myths: 210 Poems* won a number of major prizes. His latest book is *Heart Starter* (Puncher and Wattmann, Sydney, and BlazeVox, Buffalo, 2015). He is the founding editor of *Jacket magazine* and of *JPR* at poeticsrearch.com, and he has a journal at johntranter.net and a homepage at johntranter.com.

SARAH VINCENT has been published in *The Victorian Writer* and *Gargouille*. She works at Writers Victoria and is studying in RMIT's PWE program. In 2014 she was accepted into a Varuna focus-week for her memoir project *Death by Dim Sim*.

Wayside Chapel, Sydney visitors, **ROBERT HANNAH** and **TRINITY MORRIS** have both kindly given permission for their pieces to be included in this anthology.

Editors

KIRSTEN TRANTER is the author of the novels *A Common Loss* (2012) and *The Legacy* (2010), and a co-founder of the Stella Prize. Her short fiction appears in *Best Australian Stories 2014*, *Island*, and numerous anthologies, and her third novel is forthcoming in 2016. Kirsten grew up in Sydney and now lives in the San Francisco Bay Area.

LINDA GODFREY is an editor, judge and publicist for Spineless Wonders and works as a freelance editor. Her fiction and poetry has appeared in *Cordite*, the UTS writers' anthology *Nine Tenths Below,* other anthologies, audio anthologies by River Road Press and the Spineless Wonders anthology, *Escape.* She is the series editor and co-editor for the Spineless Wonders anthologies, *Small Wonder, Stoned Crows & other Australian Icons, Writing to the Edge* and *Flashing the Square.*

The joanne burns Award

Each year Spineless Wonders auspices an award for the best writing in the forms of prose poem and microfiction in honour of foremost Australian experimental poet, joanne burns. The award is open to people residing in Australia and to Australians living overseas. Finalists chosen by each year's judging panel are offered publication in our annual anthology alongside invited writers.

The inaugural *joanne burns Award* was held in 2011 and was judged by joanne burns who selected Charles D'Anastasi's 'Madame Bovary' as the winning entry and commended Erin Gough's 'William Shatner vows to save the Great Basin Pocket Mouse' and Clare McHugh's 'Briefly'. All three pieces, along with those of other finalists appear in *small wonder*, edited by Linda Godfrey and Julie Chevalier.

The *2012 joanne burns Award* was judged by Carol Jenkins who selected Mark O'Flynn's 'under the maw of luna park' as the winning entry and commended Richard Holt's 'bush burial', Trina Denner's 'playing outside', Stu Hatton's 'down south' and Paul Mitchell's 'The Old Man and the Pool'. The winner and finalists all appear in *Stoned Crows & other Australian Icons*, edited by Julie Chevalier and Linda Godfrey.

The *2013 joanne burns Award* was judged by Shady Cosgrove who selected Mark Smith's '10.42 to Sydenham' as the winning entry and Hilary Hewitt's 'happy' and Mark Robert's 'cities that are not Dublin' as runners-up. All three pieces, along with those of other finalists appear in *Writing to the Edge*, edited by Linda Godfrey and Ali Jane Smith.

In *2014, The joanne burns Award* was judged by Angela Meyer and Richard Holt who selected Susan McCreery's 'Hold Up' as the winning entry and Kirsten Tranter's 'Turing Test Study Guide' and Mark Smith's 'The Meteorologist's Daughter' as runners up. All three pieces, along with those of other finalists are published in *Flashing the Square*, edited by Linda Godfrey and Bronwyn Mehan.

The 2015 joanne burns Award was judged by Kirsten Tranter who selected Nick Couldwell's 'Dancing' as the winning entry. Runners up were Tim Heffernan for 'Butterflies in Iraq' and Matthew Gabriel for 'jesussaves82'. All three pieces, along with those of other finalists and invited contributors are published in *Out of Place* edited by Kirsten Tranter and Linda Godfrey.

ABOUT JOANNE BURNS

joanne burns grew up in Sydney's eastern suburbs. She worked as an English teacher in New South Wales, and for a time in London. She has taught creative writing in tertiary institutions, schools and community organisations. Her first collection of poems, *Snatch*, was published in London in 1972. Since then she has published more than a dozen further books of poetry. Her poems have appeared in numerous Australian literary journals, poetry magazines and have been set for study on the Higher School Certificate syllabus. joanne has been particularly concerned with the blurring of the distinctions between poetry and prose in her work, and has written extensively in prose poem/ microfiction forms. She has also written monologues and short futurist fictions and 'farables' (fables/ parables).Her latest collection *Brush* was published by Giramondo Poets in 2014.

Also from

Spineless Wonders

Small Wonder
prose poems & microfiction

edited by Linda Godfrey and Julie Chevalier

Here are short and clever pieces by thirty contemporary Australian writers on the eroticism of mashed potato, parenting as magic realism and a tongue-in-cheek history of the Cyclops bicycle. Includes award-winning writers Michael Farrell, Keri Glastonbury, Judith Beveridge and Peter Boyle. Features prose poems and microfiction selected by competition judge joanne burns.

Illustrated by talented young artist, Paden Hunter.

Stoned Crows
& other Australian Icons
prose poems & microfiction

edited by Linda Godfrey and Julie Chevalier

What do our best wordsmiths have to say about Australian icons? This anthology takes a fresh look at everything from the HIH collapse to crocs, Margaret Olley, bush burials and the ABC. We visit a post-apocalyptic Opera House and spend Saturday night in downtown Byron Bay. Tones range from nostalgic to sceptical, from wry to LOL. Featuring prose poems and microfiction by Mark O'Flynn, Anna Kerdijk Nicholson, Michael Sharkey, Moya Costello and many more.

Writing to the Edge
prose poems & microfiction
edited by Linda Godfrey and Ali Jane Smith

Flashing The Square
edited by Linda Godfrey & Bronwyn Mehan

This collection takes its name from an event at the Melbourne Writers Festival, where these miniature vignettes and mini-narratives were flashed on screens in Federation Square. There's a high standard of writing here across a broad range of subjects. The best contributions are full of potential and feeling: Susan McCreery's one-paragraph sketch of a service-station hold-up fills the reader with dread, and Michelle Wright's *Taken*, about a shark attack, with a kind of difficult grief. Ally Scale's *I Do* is heartbreaking and Shady Cosgrove's *Call an Ambulance* quite terrifying; for some reason the stories about unreasoning violence work best. Other contributors include such familiar names as Kirsten Tranter and A.S. Patric, as well as Angela Meyer.

Kerry Goldsworthy, SYDNEY MORNING HERALD

Spineless Wonders publications are available in print and digital format from participating bookshops and online. For further information about where to purchase our print, audio and ebooks, go to the Spineless Wonders website:

www.shortaustralianstories.com.au

www.ingramcontent.com/pod-product-compliance
Lightning Source LLC
Chambersburg PA
CBHW031252210726
48287CB00003B/1009